Pinocchio

tiger tales

To Sarah ~ A. B.

To my nephews, Arthur & Wilf ~ R. W.

tiger tales
5 River Road, Suite 128, Wilton, CT 06897
Published in the United States 2019
Originally published in Great Britain 2019
by Little Tiger Press Ltd.
Text adapted by Anna Bowles
Text copyright © 2019 Anna Bowles
Illustrations copyright © 2019 Richard Watson
ISBN-13: 978-1-68010-160-7
ISBN-10: 1-68010-160-9
Printed in China
LTP/1400/2621/0319

For more insight and activities, visit us at www.
tigertalesbooks.com

FAIRY TALE CLASSICS

Pinocchio

adapted by Anna Bowles

Illustrated by
Richard Watson

tiger tales

One day, Geppetto the old carpenter decided to make a puppet. He worked very skillfully, and when the puppet was finished, it looked like it was alive. Its mouth opened . . . and it stuck out its tongue. "THFFFFT!" Pinocchio *was* alive!

Pinocchio cried, "You look **boring**. I want to
see the world!" The naughty puppet ran outside—
SMACK! into a pair of legs.

"What's going on?" grumbled the policeman. "Is that man chasing you?"

"Yes! He's a robber," Pinocchio lied.

Then a very strange thing happened. Pinocchio's nose began to grow . . . .

Meanwhile, Geppetto was taken to jail!

Pinocchio sat at home feeling very pleased with himself. Suddenly, he heard a little voice . . . .

Chirp, chirp!

"I am Talking Cricket!" he said. "I will give you some advice to help you become a real boy.

Be good and kind and always do what adults tell you . . . ."

Kind old Geppetto forgave Pinocchio for sending him to jail.

"How do I become a real boy?" Pinocchio asked.

"You will need to go to school," said Geppetto kindly.

"Oh," Pinocchio sighed.
That sounded like no fun at all.

"I'll go!" Pinocchio promised. But as he spoke,
his nose grew longer and longer . . . .

Geppetto sold his coat so he could buy Pinocchio a book for school. Pinocchio was so grateful that he decided to go to school after all.

But on the way, he saw a sign . . . .

Pinocchio sold his book and bought a ticket.
"I've come to play!" he announced to the puppets.

They high-fived
and danced all day.

It was dark when Pinocchio left the theater.

"Be careful!" warned the other puppets. But Pinocchio thought he was so clever that he had nothing to be scared of.

Pinocchio was stopped by two horrible robbers.

Hello...

...little puppet.

"Don't hurt me. I don't have any money!" Pinocchio cried.

At last, Pinocchio escaped. He ran until he reached a little house.

A kind fairy lived in the house.
She put Pinocchio to bed,
where he tossed and turned.
"I'm sick!" he groaned.

The fairy brought
him some medicine.
"That looks horrible!
I won't drink it!"
"Yes, you will!"
"No, I won't!"
"Yes, you WILL!"
"What if I don't?"
"You'll die."
Sometimes, it's a good
idea to do what adults say.

Sometimes . . . .

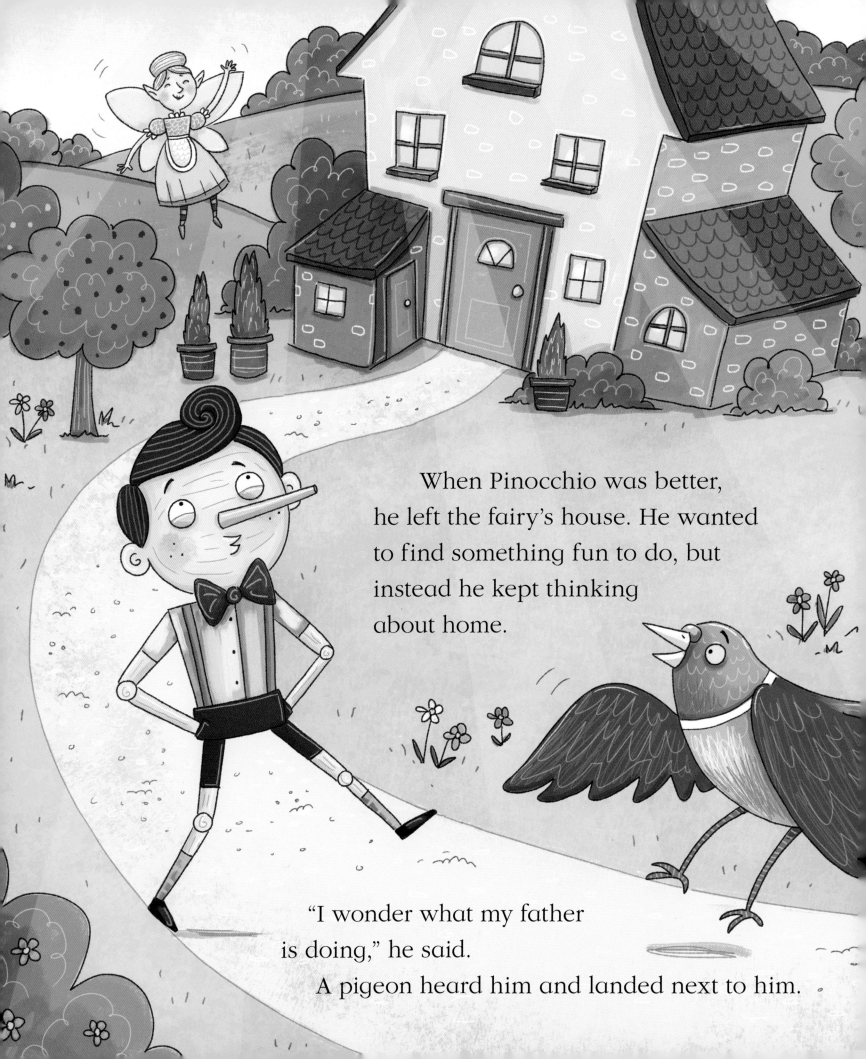

When Pinocchio was better, he left the fairy's house. He wanted to find something fun to do, but instead he kept thinking about home.

"I wonder what my father is doing," he said.

A pigeon heard him and landed next to him.

I've seen your father searching for you. He's very worried!

"I don't care!" Pinocchio snapped.

But to his amazement, his nose grew longer . . .

and longer . . . and longer!

He *did* care about Geppetto. Very much.

"I saw Geppetto rowing across the ocean to look for you," said the pigeon.

"Can you tell him I'm here?" asked Pinocchio.

"You can tell him yourself," the pigeon replied, scooping Pinocchio onto his back and flying off.

"Whoaaaaa!"

Pinocchio peered down at the ocean below. He saw . . .

a floating oar . . .

Geppetto's empty boat . . .

and a

HUGE SHARK!

"FATHER!" cried Pinocchio.

He wiggled so much that he fell off the pigeon.

Pinocchio tumbled into the ocean.

First he sank

down . . .

then rocketed up . . .

then tumbled down . . .
and was gobbled up
by the shark!

Eeek!

And what did
he see in the shark's
stomach?

Geppetto!
Pinocchio and his father hugged.

"I'm afraid we're trapped," said Geppetto. "Even if we escape from the shark, I'll drown."

Pinocchio laughed.
"I'm made of wood! I can float you to shore."

They crept up
the shark's throat.
Pinocchio reached out
to tickle its nose . . . .

AAAAACHOOOO!

They were free!

When they made it to the shore,
Pinocchio was too tired to walk.
Geppetto carried him home,
and they slept next to each other
all night.

When he woke up, Pinocchio cried,
"Father, are you all right?"

"Yes, my son," said Geppetto. "And look
what has happened to you."

While Pinocchio was asleep, he had
transformed. Smiling in the mirror, he
saw a good, kind, amazing . . .

REAL boy!

Anna Bowles

Anna is a writer and editor of children's books who has
adapted several fairy tales for the Fairy Tale Classics series.
She lives in London, England, with her husband, her collection
of fluffy hippos, her books, and a large supply of chocolate.
If she was a fairy tale character, she would probably be
the trombone player from the Fairy Tale Classics title
Beauty and the Beast.

Richard Watson

Richard grew up in a small village in North Lincolnshire, England.
He studied illustration at Lincoln University School of Art and Design
and began working as an illustrator soon after leaving the university
in 2003. Richard uses a range of techniques to produce artwork,
mixing traditional drawing and painting with collage
and mixed media. He also loves visiting galleries,
watching movies, and listening to music.